JUST PLAIN BOB

Erotica

Fifteen Minutes

of

Ass, Legs and other Kinks

Hot and Kinky

WARNING

This book contains sexually explicit scenes and adult language. It may be considered offensive to some readers. This book is for sale to adults ONLY.

Please store your files wisely where they cannot be accessed by underage readers.

* * * * * * * * * * * * * * * * * * *

WANT FREE COPIES OF MY BOOKS?

Just visit my blog and download free copies of my books:

awesomeauthors.org/justplainbob

About the Publisher

4Fun Publishing, a member of **BLVNP Incorporated**, 340 S. Lemon #6200, Walnut CA 91789, info@blvnp.com / legal@blvnp.com
NOTE: Due to the highly emotional reaction of some people to works of erotic fiction, any email sent to the above address that contains foul language or religious references is automatically deleted by our anti-spam software and will not be seen. All other communications are welcome.

DISCLAIMER

EROTICA
Fifteen Minutes of Ass, Legs and other Kinks
Hot and Kinky

By: Just Plain Bob

© **Just Plain Bob 2015**
ISBN: 978-1-68030-603-3

I rolled out of bed, and God did my head hurt. But then why wouldn't it? I have been drunk the whole weekend. As I stumbled into the bathroom, I was glad that weekends like the one I'd just managed to survive were not the norm. In fact, I hadn't had one like it since my last college frat party and that was over seven years ago. I opened the medicine cabinet, found the aspirin, took four and chased them with a glass of water.

As I was putting the bottle back, out of the corner of my eye I saw the brassiere hanging over the edge of the dirty clothes hamper and I felt the flash of anger again. I fought it down, why get upset over something that was over and done with? As I walked back into the bedroom, I saw the bed and had to fight down the anger again. I could never have slept on those sheets if I hadn't been too drunk to know what I was doing.

I went out into the kitchen and got a couple of garbage bags. I stripped the sheets and pillow cases off the bed and stuffed then into the garbage bags and then I went through the apartment and gathered up everything of hers that I could find and consigned it all to the trash bags. I set them outside the apartment door and I'd leave them there for twenty-four hours. If she hasn't picked them up by then, I'd toss them into the dumpster.

I put the coffee on to brew while I showered and dressed and then had a cup with two pieces of toast. I probably should have eaten something a little more substantial, but I was afraid I wouldn't be able to keep it down. I filled my travel mug with coffee, grabbed my briefcase and headed out the door to go to work. As soon as I hit the parking lot, the day that had started out with a bad head got worse. My car was gone. For a fleeting moment I thought it had been stolen, but then I realized that it was still sitting in the parking lot at Brady's Roadhouse and Tavern. Some Good Samaritan had kept me from driving and had seen to it that I got home. I'd have to find out who and thank him.

The cab showed up fairly quickly and it managed to get me to work with just minutes to spare. During the cab ride, I had time to lean back, stare out the window and think about the last four days and what had led up to them.

* * *

Once every three months, my company rents one of the ballrooms at the Hilton, throws a cocktail party and invites all of our customers and suppliers. The purpose of the party was basically social. The owner of the company believed that meeting socially with the people you did business with, both as buyer and seller, allowed us to have a better feel for each other and that allowed us to build easier relationships with the people we interacted with on a daily basis. It seemed to work.

These parties were an "all hands on deck" affair as far as the employees at my company were concerned. You had to be there and no excuse other than a death in the family was acceptable and even then it needed to be a very close relative.

It was at one of these cocktail parties that I met Misty. She came as the date of one of the purchasing agents for Apex Industries and when I first saw her, she took my breath away. About five feet six (and most of it appeared to be legs), a hundred and twenty pounds and all of it in the right places and she had jet black hair down to the middle of her back and the greenest eyes I'd ever seen.

As far as the cocktail party was concerned, I may as well have been alone in a crater on the far side of the moon. I don't recall a single word anyone said to me at that party. Outside of Misty and her date, I don't even remember anyone else who was there. I spent the entire party moving around to keep Misty in sight - I just could not take my eyes off of her.

The amazing thing is that at no time during that party were we introduced and by the time the party started breaking up, we had not spoken one word to each other. I was at one of the side tables getting a cup of black coffee for the road when someone moved up beside me and I felt a slight tug on my jacket pocket. I looked over and saw Misty standing next to me and I saw her hand coming out of my pocket. She looked up at me, winked, got a cup of coffee and walked away. She rejoined her date and they left the party. I must have stood there a full minute wondering if I had really seen her wink at me and then I remembered her hand coming out of my pocket. I reached in the pocket and felt a piece of paper and I pulled it out and looked at it. It had some printing on it and I read:

"Misty - 555-1237 - after 6 PM."

The next day, 6 PM couldn't come quick enough for me. At 5:59:48 on my digital watch, I punched in the number she had given me and at 6:00:02 the phone was answered and a female voice said:

"Hello?"

"Misty? This is…"

"I know who you are, Mr. Big Eyes, and I have a question for you. What do you want?"

"You!"

"I haven't eaten yet so maybe you could take me to dinner and we can talk about why you want me and why I should give you what you want. My address is 222 Monaco, apartment 2C."

"I'm on the way."

Twenty minutes later, I was ringing her doorbell and she answered the door, purse in hand. "My mother won't let me go out with strangers and I don't know you."

"My name is Rob."

"And I'm Misty so I guess we aren't strangers any more. Where are you taking me?"

"Do you like Italian?"

"As a matter of fact, I do."

As we pulled out of the parking lot she asked, "So Mr. Rob Big Eyes, why didn't you introduce yourself to me last night?"

"Because you were with Jack Towers and I have to work closely with him. He would have immediately known that my reason for walking up to the two of you wasn't to talk with him and that just might have soured our working relationship."

"Jack is an old friend and I was only there with him because he needed some 'arm candy' for the event. He wouldn't have minded at all."

I took her to Mario's and we talked and got to know each other as we ate and sipped wine. She kissed me on the cheek when I took her back to her apartment and she told me to call. I did and we had three dates and at the end of the third one, when I walked her to her door, she gave me the most passionate kiss I'd ever received in my life and then she grabbed my tie and pulled me through the door and into her apartment.

As soon as the door was closed, she turned and moved into my arms and her lips met mine. I felt her tongue flick out and I let her feel the tip of mine. She sucked my tongue into her mouth and ground her pelvis into my hard cock and she moaned:

"I want you."

Her fingers started on my shirt buttons and I picked her up and asked her which way to the bedroom and she pointed the way and I carried her there and set her down on the bed. As I stripped off my clothes she pulled the spread and the blanket out of the way and then took off her panties. She got on the bed and pulled her dress up to her waist and then pulled her knees back.

"Please baby," she moaned, "Hurry, I need it."

I moved between her legs and started to ease my hard cock into her. She was tight, but she was wet and inch by inch I pushed in.

"Oh yes, oh yes baby, do it, push hard."

I got all of me in and I started out stroking slowly in and back and she cried:

"Oh God yes! Fuck me, lover, fuck me" and I made my strokes longer and pushed in deeper as she encouraged me. She started humping up at me and I increased the tempo and started fucking her harder. The strokes were hard and deep and she was whining:

"I need it, oh God I need it. Make me cum, lover, make me cum."

And then her nails bit into my back and she uttered a guttural sound as her body shook and trembled. I could feel her pussy clutching my cock and I let go what was possibly the biggest load of my life. Her arms went around my neck and she pulled me down and kissed me and then said:

"That was stupendous, lover. Can we do this every night?"

I smiled at her and said that yes we could.

"Could we do it again now? Can I take my clothes off and we'll do it again?"

I smiled and said, "It might be a while. I'll need a little time to recharge."

"Oh I can help you there, lover" and she shifted her body and her mouth swallowed the head of my cock. She took several sucks on it and then she took her mouth off me and said, "We taste marvelous together, baby. Just let me get my clothes off and I'll get back to it."

She did get back to it twice more that night and I fell asleep in her bed.

* * *

After that I saw her every night and every night she reduced me to a smoldering ruin. After six months of basically going steady, I asked her to marry me and she said:

"Maybe, lover, but I don't know that I'm ready for that yet. How about we have a trial period?"

"A trial period?"

"Yes, baby, why don't we try living together and see how that goes."

She moved in with me and for six months everything seemed to be going very well.

Until last Thursday evening.

I had been on a short business trip and was due back on Friday. I finished up sooner than expected and was able to catch the last flight out on Thursday. I didn't bother to call ahead because Misty told me she would be having dinner with her mother and sister that night and I didn't expect her to be home.

But she was home.

I noticed the trail of discarded men's and women's clothing leading from the front door to the bedroom at the same time I heard:

"Oh God yes! Harder, damn you, harder, fuck me harder."

I dropped my suitcase on the floor and walked over and looked in the bedroom. Some guy I had never seen before was pounding his cock into Misty. Her legs were up on his shoulders, her hands were clutching at the sheets and her head rolled from side to side as she moaned:

"Fuck me, oh shit, fuck me."

I had always thought of myself as a calm, laid back sort of guy, someone who could handle problems and pressure, but right then I lost it. I just plain lost it. I stomped over to the bed, grabbed a handful of the guy's hair, jerked his head back and then hit him in the face as hard as I could. I pulled him off Misty and threw him against the wall. I saw his head bounce off the wall as he slid down to the floor. Misty didn't even know I was in the room until the guy's dick was jerked out of her. She whined:

"Oh no, don't stop" and then her eyes opened and she saw me and screamed as she tried to cover up. I pointed a finger at her and snarled:

"Get your fucking ass dressed and get out of here. Do it now!"

I walked over to the guy who was lying on the floor shaking his head and grabbed him by the ankles and dragged him out of the apartment. I gathered up his clothes and tossed them out the door and then went back to the bedroom. Misty had gone into the bathroom and I don't know if she locked herself in or not. I didn't trust myself to try to open the door. I leaned my head against the door and yelled:

"I'm leaving for thirty minutes. Be gone when I get back and make sure you leave your key on the kitchen table."

It was closer to an hour before I got back and she was gone. I went into work the next morning and somehow made it through the day. After work, I went out to have a few drinks with some of the people I work with and ended up on a tear that lasted all weekend.

* * *

When I got to my desk I turned on my computer and clicked on the mail icon. I had forty-one messages and I started wading through them, moving the important ones into the proper folders for later perusal and deleting the junk. I came to one that was from "Little Miss Sweet Cheeks" and the subject was "For Rob's eyes only." I opened it and there was a short message and an attachment. The message said:

"You are well rid of the cheating slut. How about this for a replacement?"

The attachment was a photo of a fantastic heart shaped ass with the two cheeks split by a thong made out of a string of pearls. I looked around the office to see if anyone was looking my way. I half expected to see a grinning woman casting glances my way, but everyone else in the office was head down and busy at work and I didn't see a soul paying attention to me.

A little deductive reasoning on my part told me that the sender of the e-mail had to have been among the people at the bar Friday night when I blabbed to the world about the faithless bitch that I was going to marry. It also told me that it was a co-worker because who else would have my office e-mail address? I tried to remember which of women I worked with were at the bar Friday, but the night was too hazy a memory. Then I had a thought. Maybe it wasn't a woman. Maybe it was one of the guys I worked with and he was having some fun pulling my chain.

I pushed the matter aside and got busy doing what they paid me to do. But when I took my coffee break I took another look at the photo and then decided to do something that for me that was way out. I typed up a message and sent it off to Little Miss Sweet Cheeks.

"Nice ass, Sweet Cheeks, but I'm a leg man."

After work I caught a ride over to the Roadhouse to pick up my car. I stayed for one drink and then, not really wanting to go home, I went out for a bite to eat. When I got home the garbage bags were gone and there was a note from Misty taped to my door.

"Please call me on my cellphone. I need to talk to you."

I wadded it up and tossed it away.

Tuesday at work there was another e-mail with an attachment from Little Miss Sweet Cheeks.

"I wouldn't dream of offering you less than the total package."

The attachment was a waist-down photo showing a sexy a pair of legs. She was wearing thigh highs and a pair of CFMs with what looked to be four-inch heels. Did the legs belong to the same body that had the fantastic ass? I had no way of knowing for sure, but whoever the lady was, she was wearing what appeared to be the same pearl thong.

There were at least eighty women scattered in the five floors of our building and while I had never met all of them, I would have thought for sure, being the leg man that I am, I would have noticed legs like that. Unless the lady always wore slacks I should have noticed them entering or leaving the building, walking the halls, in the cafeteria or waiting in the lobby for the elevator. Those thoughts brought me back to the idea that one of the guys I worked with was pulling my leg.

Several times during the morning, I went back and looked at the photos of Sweet Cheeks. At lunch I looked closely at every woman in the cafeteria trying to find a hint that one of them could be LMSC, but I came up with nothing. I did see a dozen or so ladies I would have liked to take home with me for some further investigation, but none I could match to the photos on my computer.

Just before quitting time, I composed an e-mail to Sweet Cheeks. "Do we work for the same company? If so I can't believe I don't recognize those legs."

I left my desk ten minutes early and loitered in the lobby to check out the ladies as they left the building to go home. I saw dozens that I would have loved to take off to the side and ask them to strip and show me their butts and legs, but not one that I could say for sure was Little Miss Sweet Cheeks. The more I thought about it the more I came to believe that I was the butt of some practical joke.

* * *

I hit Safeway on the way home and picked up a small steak and the fixings for a salad. I planned on a quiet evening with a book, but when I pulled into the parking lot at the apartments I saw Misty's red Mustang parked there so I did a quick u-turn and went and found a restaurant where I ate dinner. Then I went to a sports bar and nursed a couple of beers while watching a ball game on TV. I went home around midnight and Misty's car was gone.

In the thirty-six e-mails waiting for me the next morning, one was from Sweet Cheeks.

"I've been there all along, just waiting for you to notice me."

Attached was a waist down photo from behind of that fantastic ass, those gorgeous legs and the ever present pearl thong. Her e-mail address wasn't an in-house one; and, if she were real, I wondered if she accessed it from work during the day. One way to find out, I thought; and I fired off an e-mail to her.

"If you are waiting for me to notice then you should know you've got my attention. Obviously I don't know who you are so you have to make the next move."

I kept checking my e-mail during that day, but nothing came in from Sweet Cheeks.

Misty's Mustang was in the parking lot at the apartments so I spent another evening eating out, drinking in a sports bar and watching ballgames on TV.

* * *

The next morning there was a response from Sweet Cheeks.

"I've been lusting after you since the first time I saw you in the cafeteria. You won't believe some of the fantasies I've had of us. You, sitting on a stool in the men's room while I straddle you and take you deep in me. On the large table in the conference room with my legs up on your broad shoulders as you push your hard cock into me. In the copier room, bent forward over the copy machine, skirt up around my waist, panties down around my ankles as you thrust your hard cock into me.

"I stood behind you in the elevator last week and just looking at your strong back and thinking of what you could do to me had my pussy so wet that my panties were soaked."

The attached photo was of a very wet pussy and underneath were the words, "See what you do to me?"

I stared at the photo and then sent off a quick reply.

"That is nothing compared to what you are doing to me. When are you going to step forward so we can take this to the next level?"

Since I'd received no response during the day to other e-mails I'd sent, I assumed that she didn't check her messages until she got home so I didn't expect to hear from her until the next day so I was surprised when there was an e-mail from her at three that afternoon.

"That you want to meet me has my heart pounding and my pussy is wet at just the thought. In fact, the knowledge that you want to meet with me had me so hot I had to sneak off to the ladies' room. I took a stall and locked the door. I slid my panties down and removed them and then I attacked my wet pussy. I rubbed my clit with my left hand while working a finger from my right inside. My pussy was hot and wet and I'm so glad I was alone in the room so that my moans weren't heard. Soon I had three fingers plunging into me as far as they would go and as I fingered myself in my mind I saw myself bent over your desk as you thrust your rock-hard cock hard and deep into me.

"After I put my panties back on, I debated walking past your desk, but I was afraid you would smell the desire on me and I don't know if I am ready yet for you to know who I am."

I considered that for the rest of the afternoon and then just before I went home, I sent:

"If you aren't ready why did you even start this?"

When I got home I scoped out the parking lot and didn't see Misty's car so for the first night that week, I didn't have to eat out. I had just finished washing my dinner dishes when the phone rang. I wiped my hands off with the dish towel and answered it.

"Hello?"

"Hi."

"What do you want, Misty?"

"You."

"You had me, Misty, but apparently I wasn't enough."

"That isn't true Rob. I need to talk to you. Can I come over?"

"No Misty, you can't come over. I can't see that we have anything that needs discussing."

"Please, Rob, just give me fifteen minutes."

"I don't think so, Misty; goodbye."

As I hung up the phone, I wondered what she could possibly have wanted to say, but not enough to listen.

* * *

Friday's e-mail from Sweet Cheeks said, "I'm ready. I'm just not sure that you are. Are you totally over the slut yet? I want you, but I don't want to catch you on the rebound where you are just looking for someone so you can prove to yourself that you are still a desirable guy."

I leaned back in my chair and thought about that. I hadn't given that any conscious thought, but did I feel that I was lacking in something? Was Misty's betrayal because I was somehow inadequate? Did I need to prove that I was still a desirable guy? I didn't think so, but then what guy with a normal ego would? Maybe I did need to have that talk with Misty.

The other thought that Sweet Cheek's e-mail provoked was that the e-mail sure didn't sound like something a guy would write. Could I be wrong in thinking that it was a guy I worked with pulling my leg? Was there really a Sweet Cheeks?

I spent a quiet evening at home and went to bed early. When I woke up in the morning, I laid in bed staring up at the ceiling and wondering what to do with my two days off. Discounting the prior weekend when I had gone off, I'd not had a weekend alone in almost a ten months.

The weather was good so after breakfast I grabbed my golf clubs and headed for the municipal golf course to see if I could hook up with someone looking to fill out a foursome. I got lucky and managed to play a decent eighteen and the guys I hooked up with said they played every Saturday and Sunday and asked me if I would care to join them, and I said I'd love to.

I stopped on the way home and did my grocery shopping for the coming week. When I got to the apartment, I saw Misty's Mustang parked there, but this time I couldn't do a u-turn and take off because I had frozen food, including two half gallons of ice cream, that I had to get into the apartment and into the icebox. I parked and started to get the groceries out of my car. I kept one eye on Misty's car, expecting her to get out and come over to me. She just sat there. It took me two trips to get everything into the apartment, but Misty never left her car.

I put everything away and then went to the front window and pulled the curtain aside and looked out. Misty was still sitting there. I fixed myself a sandwich for dinner and then sat down in front of the TV and jumped channels for maybe twenty minutes, but I just couldn't get into anything. I got up and went back to the window and looked out to see that Misty was still sitting there in her car.

I went back to the couch and picked up the book I'd been reading, but I couldn't get into it. Every fifteen or twenty minutes, I was back at the window looking out and every time, the red Mustang was still sitting there. Half a dozen times I had my hand on the door knob, ready to go out there and ask Misty just what the hell was going on, but I knew that is what she wanted so each time I pulled back. I checked one last time before going to bed and she was still there.

In the morning, Misty was gone and after fixing myself some breakfast, I grabbed my clubs and headed out to meet the guys I had played with on Saturday. Misty was in the parking lot when I got home, but I ignored her and walked right by her car on my way to the apartment. I took a shower, dressed and then called around to see if anything was going on that I would be interested in. My friend Brad steered me to a party at Phil's place and I left the apartment and headed for Phil's.

There were a dozen people there that I knew and I was having a good time. It got better when Betty Jean pulled me into a bedroom, locked the door behind us and then lifted her skirt and took off her thong. I was a little hesitant because she was the girlfriend of a guy I know. She saw the look on my face and said:

"We both need this, Rob. I caught Steve fucking Marsha Meers and you caught Misty. We need to burn the two of them out of our systems even if it is only for one night."

"You are still wearing his engagement ring."

"I'll give it back to him when I tell him I got even with him." She saw the look on my face and quickly said, "I'm not going to tell him with whom."

"I love it from behind, Robbie" she said as she lifted her skirt and pulled off her panties. She leaned forward over the bed and braced herself with her hands.

"Do me, Robbie, do me hard. Fuck me, Robbie, fuck me hard and burn the memory of Steve right out of me."

I'd like to say that we did indeed burn our exes out of our systems, but as hot a fuck as Betty Jean was and as much as I enjoyed it, I couldn't help but think that she didn't even come close to being as good as Misty.

Who was still sitting in my parking lot when I got home at midnight.

I gave up the fight. I walked over to her car and she rolled the window down.

"What the hell are you doing, Misty?"

"I want to talk to you, Rob. I figure if I hang around sooner or later you will give me fifteen minutes of your time."

"Not likely, Misty. You know that this could be considered stalking right? I could get a restraining order and if you kept it up I could have you arrested."

"Oh come on, Rob. You would have to hire a lawyer, pay court costs for things like filing fees and you would have to waste half a day doing it. You would go to all that trouble just to keep from giving me fifteen minutes?"

"Give it up, Misty. By your choice it is over."

I walked away, but an hour later I looked just before I went to bed and she was still there.

* * *

There were fifty-one e-mails waiting for me Monday morning when I got to work, but I ignored fifty of them and went straight to the one that said From: Little Miss Sweet Cheeks, Subject: Weekend.

"Did you think about me this weekend? I thought about you - a lot! So much so that I almost wore my poor fingers to the bone."

There was an attached photo of a very wet looking pussy (have I mentioned that Sweet Cheeks is shaved?) and underneath it were the words:

"This is what I look like after a session of thinking of you."

I immediately typed and sent, "I'm ready! Hell, I'm more than ready. Stop tormenting me and let's do it!"

I was about half-way through the other fifty e-mails when the little box popped up on the lower right corner of my screen.

"New message in your MSN mailbox from Little Miss Sweet Cheeks Re: Okay."

I clicked on it and read the one word message, "Okay." I thought about sending the reply, "Okay what?" but then decided to just wait and see what Sweet Cheeks would do next. The day flew by as I buried myself in my latest project and at quitting time, I joined the exodus toward the elevator. I wasn't paying attention to who was waiting for the elevator, when it got there, we all crowded in. As it started down, I felt a hand on my ass and I turned and saw Brenda Thomas smiling at me. The elevator was too crowded to say anything so I turned to face forward and as I did, Brenda gave my butt cheek a little squeeze.

My God! Brenda Thomas! No way I would have even remotely thought of her being Little Miss Sweet Cheeks. But then why would I? I had never seen her in anything but a pantsuit and I couldn't ever recall seeing her in a pair of heels and (a dark cloud suddenly appeared as I remembered) she was married!

A hundred thoughts banged around in my head as the elevator slowly descended toward the lobby. Chief among them were the thoughts of why a married woman is lusting after me? Was her husband one of those guys who got off on his wife being with another man? Was he the one who took the photos? Was Brenda one of those women who ran around behind her husband's back? The bottom line was "Did I want to have an affair with a married woman?" and the answer was "No."

As soon as the door opened out onto the lobby, I stepped out of the elevator and moved to one side to get out of the way of everyone heading for the front door. Brenda moved next to me and said:

"Surprised?"

"Very. Tell me, what does a married lady want with me?"

"I'm not married anymore and as far as what do I want from you? How about my chimes rung loud and often. Your place or a motel?"

"Why not your place?"

"The marriage might be over but the kids remain and I don't want to do anything nasty with them and the sitter in the house."

"Are you sure about this?"

"You've seen the photos and read the e-mails so what do you think?"

"You want to ride with me and come back for your car later or are you going to follow me?"

"No need to follow you, honey, I know where you live. Come on, race you."

The red Mustang was sitting there when I pulled in and parked. I sat in my car and looked at Misty parked there as I waited for Brenda. When the Expedition pulled in and parked next to me, I got out and then holding hands with Brenda, I walked by the Mustang and into the apartment. As soon as the door closed Brenda turned to me and gave me a passionate kiss and then she said:

"You have no idea how much I want this. How about no talk for now, just get me into your bedroom. We can talk later."

In the bedroom we both quickly stripped. I was naked first and I stepped forward and started pulling her panties down as she was unhooking her bra. Her panties were soaking wet and I brought them to my nose and sniffed them. The aroma lit my fire and I picked her up and laid her down on the bed. I dove between her legs and pressed my mouth against her dripping pussy. I sucked and licked and shoved my tongue inside her and she pushed her hips up at my face and had an orgasm.

My cock was throbbing as I moved up between her spread legs and pushed my cock into her hot slit. My cock slid into her like a hot knife through a stick of butter and she let out a groan and her legs came up and locked around me. I started fucking her hard, trying to shove myself deeper and deeper into her. She moaned, she cried and her hands clutched at me as she had another orgasm. "Oh shit!" she screamed as she shook and trembled and that pushed me over the edge and I fired my load up into her belly.

With my soft cock still inside her we held each other and kissed, our tongues fighting with each other. I felt my cock twitch and she must have felt it too because she pushed me away and moved her body so she could take my cock in her mouth. My cock twitched and twitched and slowly started to grow and as soon as it was hard enough to suit her she moved over me and lowered herself down as she guided me into her. She pushed down hard until it was pubic bone against pubic bone and then she rode me.

She raised and lowered herself and rocked back and forth. Her nails dug into my chest as she moaned and cried. She whispered:

"Are you glad, baby? Are you glad I sent you my pictures? Did you like looking at my ass, baby? Did looking at my ass make you hard?"

It went on for several more minutes and then we came together and she rolled off me and her hand went down to my limp cock and she started fondling it. I pushed her hand away and muttered, "Greedy bitch" and she laughed and said:

"I've waited a long time for this, baby. I want it."

"And you can have it, but you will have to wait. I'm not that quick when it comes to recovering."

"That's okay, baby, as long as you do recover."

I got up and fixed us a light supper and when we finished it Brenda said, "Is dessert ready yet?"

It wasn't, but her hot mouth took care of that problem. When it was over and we were lying there Brenda said:

"It was everything I hoped it would be, lover, and I wish I could stay the night, but I need to get home to my kids. The sitter has to leave by ten. That's the latest I can stay during the week. My parents love having the kids so I'll arrange for them to watch the kids this weekend and we can have more time. Can I use your shower?"

"Of course."

As she was getting ready to leave, she said that tomorrow night was Jessica's recital at school so tomorrow night would be out and next day was parent's night at the school.

"Can you hold out for two days, or will you have forgotten me by then?"

"It will be tough, but I'll try to manage."

I walked her out to her Expedition and watched her pull out of the lot and I wondered what Misty was thinking as she watched it happen. In fact, I wondered why she was even still there after having seen me take Brenda into the apartment. Not enough to ask though. I went back inside and slept like a baby.

* * *

The next day at work, there was an e-mail from Sweet Cheeks. I opened it and all there was was one word, "Thanks." No attachment, but then I really didn't need one anymore since I had seen the total package. It was going to be hard for me to wait two days to see Brenda again. I buried myself in my current project and the day moved quickly by. I ate lunch at my desk so I could stay on top of the project and it wasn't until around three in the afternoon that I got up to go to the cafeteria and get a Coke. I was walking down the hall and I saw Brenda walking toward me and my cock sprang to attention. Yep, it was definitely going to be a bitch waiting two more days. As Brenda came up alongside me, she reached out and grabbed my arm and pulled me toward her. I saw that we were just outside the supply room and she opened the door and pulled me inside.

"I can't wait two days, lover," she said as she shoved her slacks down. She bent over a stack of cartons and said, "Hurry, baby, hurry."

I unzipped, took out my cock and as she spread her legs and pulled her cheeks apart I moved behind her and I one hard push I was in her. She hissed, "Yes, oh yes" and pushed back at me and I started fucking her. She took the lid off of a carton and put it in her mouth and bit down on it so she wouldn't make noise and I pounded into her. Several minutes went by and Brenda had two orgasms before I shot my wad and then we hurriedly got presentable. As she was getting ready to open the door she said:

"Same time, same place tomorrow?"

I nodded a yes and she opened the door and peeked out. "All clear" she said and we got back to work.

Misty was in the parking lot when I got home and I breezed right by her without looking at her and went into the apartment. That night I didn't even look outside once to see if Misty was still parked there.

* * *

The next day at work was a carbon copy of the day before except it took me a few more minutes to get Brenda and myself off. As she was leaving the supply room, Brenda said:

"I plan on leaving work two hours early tomorrow. That will give us more time before I have to be home. All right with you?"

I told her that it was and that I was looking forward to it. That night I was in such a good mood that I smiled and waved at Misty as I walked by her Mustang. Bad move! The phone rang two minutes after I got inside the apartment and it was Misty.

"Did that mean a thaw?" she asked. "Are you going to give me my fifteen minutes?"

"No, Misty, all it meant was that I was in a damned good mood. Right up until you called. Leave me alone, Misty."

"Not until I get my fifteen minutes."

"Good luck on that" I said as I hung up.

It was a wonder that I got anything at all done the next day what with all the time I spent with my eyes on the clock. Two minutes before my normal quitting time, I was up and on the way out of the building. Brenda was already there when I got to the apartment. There was no sign of Misty, but then she didn't expect me home for another two hours. Once in the apartment, Brenda and I raced for the bedroom.

It was a repeat of our first night together. We fucked, did a sixty-nine and then fucked again. As we lay there recovering from our second bout and as she fondled my cock she said:

"You know, baby, it was my ass that started this and you still haven't had a taste of it."

My cock twitched and she giggled and said, "I think I touched a nerve there. You want my ass, baby? You want to push your hard cock deep into my ass and see how tight and hot it is? I love taking cock in my ass baby."

As she talked she fondled me and my cock started coming back to life and as it grew in her hand she exclaimed:

"You do! You want to push your dick into my shitter. You want to get nasty with me. Oh God, baby, I'm getting hot just thinking of you stirring my shit with your dick. I want your nice clean cock in my nasty ass."

"You filthy slut" I growled as I got out of bed to go get the KY Jelly. She laughed and said, "You love it, you dirty old man."

I spent some time working her asshole with my lubed up fingers until she moaned:

"Enough with the foreplay damn it, stuff my ass."

I pushed into her and she hissed, "Oh fucking yes, oh God yes. Hard, baby, fuck my ass hard."

She had her head down on a pillow and was moaning, "Fuck my ass, fuck my ass, fuck my ass" as I gripped her hips and pounded Little Miss Sweet Cheeks as hard as I could. It was a new thing for me. Every other woman I'd had anal sex with kept saying, "Take it slow, easy, go easy" but not Brenda. Brenda kept asking for it harder and faster. I was doing the best I could and she kept moaning, "Yes, yes, yes, yes."

When I came and it triggered something in her and she had another one of those intense orgasms. It was another first for me; I had never before given a woman an anal orgasm. I pulled out and fell to the bed beside her. Her head was still on the pillow and her ass was up in the air as I asked:

"Is this going anywhere or is it just sex?"

"What's wrong with just sex?" she panted.

"Nothing. Just looking ahead."

"Let's just play it by ear for right now. I need to shower and get home to relieve the baby sitter."

She jumped out of bed and headed for the bathroom.

Brenda went in to use the shower and as soon as I heard the water running, I made a quick decision to join her. In my hurry to get off the bed, I knocked Brenda's purse off the nightstand and when it hit the floor a bunch of stuff spilled out. I bent down and picked up everything and put it back on the nightstand and then I sat there and stared at the purse. Among the items I'd picked up off the floor were a wedding and engagement ring. If Brenda wasn't married any more why was she carrying her rings around in her purse?

On a whim I looked her up in the phone book, picked up the bedside phone and called her number. A man answered and I asked for Mr. Thomas.

"Speaking."

"Mr. Thomas, my name is Brandon Stiles and I'm calling to elicit your support for..."

"I'm sorry, but I don't deal with telephone solicitors" and he hung up on me.

I thought back to my very first e-mail from Little Miss Sweet Cheeks. "You are well rid of the cheating slut" but what was Brenda doing if not cheating? When she came out of the shower and was toweling off I said:

"Call your baby sitter and ask her if she can give you one more hour. Tell her you will double her rate if she will do it."

"I can't, lover. Tomorrow is a school day for her and her mother is quite adamant that she be home by ten. I can't come over tomorrow, but I will see you at work and we can make plans for Saturday."

As we left the apartment, I saw that the red Mustang was parked there and I wondered what Misty was thinking after seeing Brenda again.

As I climbed back into the bed that still smelled of Brenda, I thought that there could be reasons for what I'd found out. She could have the rings in her purse because she wanted them handy if she ran across a pawn shop. It would be a nice slap in the face to the ex to pawn the rings for a fraction of what he paid for them. Maybe she kept them in her purse so she could slip them on when she stopped for drinks after work with the girls thinking that they would keep the wolves away. Maybe her husband answered the phone because he had stopped by to see the kids knowing that Brenda wouldn't be there and he could avoid seeing her. The only thing I knew for sure was that I was going to have to find out. There was no percentage in having an affair with a married woman. Sooner or later she would get tired of you and dump you if her husband didn't find out and come after you first.

I laid there in bed and tried to think of how to find out. I could call the husband and flat out ask him, but that would just create problems for Brenda. I wasn't about to hire a private detective, but thinking about one gave me the idea of what I could do.

The next morning I was parked down the block from Brenda's house at six in the morning and at seven-ten, she backed her Expedition out of the garage and down the driveway and headed for work. At seven-fifteen, a man backed a Ford Taurus out of the garage and that told me all I needed to know. She was still married or she had a live-in lover. Either way, I wasn't going to be the 'other man.'

I was in the cafeteria at lunch time and Brenda joined me at my table. "I'd kiss you" she said, "But that would tell everybody that I have the hots for you. It would be true, but we don't need to get the gossips working. How do you want to handle Saturday?"

"I thought I'd play eighteen holes and then maybe catch a movie. Find a party to go to at night."

"I thought we were going to have something going on Saturday."

"I thought so to until I found out that you lied to me and are still married. I hated what Misty and some asshole did to me and I'll be damned if I'm going to cause some other poor bastard to feel the same way."

"You don't understand, Rob. I don't love him."

"Then divorce him, Brenda, but I will not knowingly cheat with another man's wife."

I got up from the table and left her sitting there.

* * *

That night I stopped after work to have a few drinks with some of the people from work and about an hour into the evening, one of the girls from purchasing asked me to dance. An hour later she had me out in the parking lot on the back seat of her car and was pleading with me to make her cum. I fucked her for a good ten minutes and gave her two orgasms and when we got out of her car and were headed back into the bar, she thanked me and said she hoped we could do it again.

"I love the orgasms I have on the back seat. Too bad my husband can't give them to me. If he could I could stay away from bars."

For the first time I looked down at her hand and saw she was wearing rings. Why hadn't I noticed it before? She saw me look and she said, "It doesn't bother you, does it? I mean all it is is sex right? You make me go boom and then I go home and make him go boom. Both sides win right?"

As I drove home, I wondered if she was right. Was it only sex? Her husband couldn't give her orgasms so she got them from someone else and then she went home and gave him an orgasm. As long as everyone got off, no harm no foul? Maybe Misty could enlighten me on the subject. She was in the parking lot when I got there and I almost talked myself into going over to her car and asking her to come in. Only almost.

Saturday I joined my new friends on the golf course and shot a fairly good eighteen and then stayed and had a few beers with them. Misty was parked in the lot when I got home and I wondered how long she was going to persist and that led me to wondering why she was persisting. The girl was spending a large chunk of her free time sitting in my parking lot and I wondered what she hoped to get out of it. Oh I know she said she wanted fifteen minutes of my time, but to what end. What did she hope to accomplish in that fifteen minutes?

I took a shower, made myself a light supper and then I called around and found that there was a party at Marty's and I headed on over there. The first people I saw when I walked in were Steve and Betty Jean. A quick glance at her finger showed me that her engagement ring was still there. She saw me and smiled and winked at me and I headed for the bar. Half an hour later, Betty Jean slipped next to me and asked me to meet her in the upstairs bathroom and then moved away.

I entered the bathroom and Betty Jean was already there. She pushed the door closed and locked it and then she lifted her skirt and bent over the sink and spread her legs.

"Hurry Rob. Hurry up and fuck me."

When I came into the room I had intended to ask about her being with Steve and about still having his ring on, but she looked so inviting that I took out my cock and slid it into her. As I fucked her I asked her about her being with Steve.

"I thought you were going to break it off with him?"

"I was" she moaned, "But when he took me home after the party, he went down on me and I had a massive orgasm knowing he was sucking you out of me. He didn't know it, he just thought I was hot and wet for him. I found out that it is a major turn on to fuck other guys and give him sloppy seconds and have him eat me out when I've got some guys cum in me. I'm getting my revenge and having the biggest orgasms of my life. Come on, baby, fuck me hard and fill me up so I can feed Steve."

I like Steve, but I had to admit that as she told me what she was doing I started to fuck her harder and faster and when I came I was thinking of Steve on his knees sucking my sauce out of Betty Jean. Of course I felt guilty as hell as soon as my dick wilted. I was one confused puppy when I left that bathroom and returned to the party. It wasn't twenty minutes later when Marty's wife Sarah came up to me and asked me if Betty Jean had left me enough strength to satisfy another and she ran her hand over my cock and told me that she would like to try me on.

"What about Marty?"

"He is so drunk right now that we could do it in front of him and he would never know it was happening."

"But why?"

"Because Marty isn't worth a shit in bed and I hear that you are."

"Where?"

"Give me ten minutes and then come upstairs to the master bedroom."

She walked away and as soon as she was out of sight I headed for the front door. As I drove home I wondered at all I had found out over the last week. I'd had sex with three different women and every one of them was cheating (well, maybe not Betty Jean - she wasn't married and Steve had cheated on her) and a fourth one had just offered to cheat with me. Add to that the woman I was going to marry cheated on me and I had to ask myself what it all meant. Was I somehow out of sync with the times? Was there something about me that yelled out "cheat with him or cheat on him - it's his lot in life?"

Misty was still in the parking lot when I got there and I suddenly decided to see if I could get some answers.

* * *

I think I surprised her when I rapped on her window. She rolled it down and I said:

"Okay, you get your fifteen minutes."

I turned and headed for my apartment. I heard the car door close and then the sound of her feet as she hurried along behind me. I left the door open when I walked inside and maybe thirty seconds later I heard it close and I turned to see Misty standing there. Cheating slut or no, she still took my breath away when I saw her. I looked at my watch and said:

"Okay, you are on the clock."

"May I sit down?"

"Go ahead."

She sat on the couch and I took the easy chair across from her.

"First" she said, "I hope you realize that I haven't spent days sitting in your parking lot just so I could have fifteen minutes to blow smoke up your ass. Whether you choose to believe it or not, Rob, nothing but the truth is going to be spoken by me. No lies and no bullshit.

"To begin with, when you asked me to marry you it was all I could do not to jump up and scream 'Yes!' I knew you were the one I wanted to spend the rest of my life with, but I also knew I wasn't ready for marriage. Probably the thing I should have done was say, 'Sorry, Rob, but I'm just not ready at this time to be tied down,' but I was afraid that if I did that you would move on. I wanted to marry you, Rob, just not right then. So to keep you around until I was ready, I suggested the living together thing.

"The reason I wasn't ready to get married just then was not that I didn't love you because I did and I do. The reason was an insatiable curiosity about what sex was like with different guys. I wanted to experience those differences. I wanted to see what big cocks were like, what small cocks were like, what fat ones and skinny ones were like. I wanted to compare whites, blacks, Asians and Little Green Men from Mars if any were around. I couldn't do that if I were married. I know me, Rob, and I know that when I say 'I do' and promise to be faithful I will do just that until the day I die. I needed to get my curiosity satisfied before I got married. I guess my first mistake was in trying to keep you close while I got it out of my system."

"What was your second?"

"What?"

"You said that keeping me close was your first mistake. What was your second?"

"Bringing him here. If we would have gone to his place or a motel you would have never found out and this time next month I would have been telling you that I was ready to get married and make us permanent."

"Why this time next month?"

"I had one more thing I wanted to do before settling down and it was set up for next week."

I wanted to ask what the last thing she wanted to do was, but at the same time I really didn't want to know.

"The guy I pulled off of you didn't look all that special to me. What was it he had that you just had to try?"

"He wasn't anything special, but he was the guy who set up what I was going to do next week and he wanted a taste."

The way she said that and the tone she used to say it made me have to ask:

"What was he setting up?"

"I was going to be the entertainment at his brother's bachelor party."

"The entertainment?"

"You know, do a strip and a couple of lap dances."

"That's it? A strip and some lap dances?"

She looked at me for several seconds and then she turned her head away and looked down at the floor as she said:

"Well, I did say no lies and no bullshit. It was going to be a gangbang."

"A gangbang? How many?"

"Seven."

"Why in God's name would you want to do a gangbang?"

"To see what it would be like. I'd done a threesome and a foursome and I wanted to see what more than three would be like."

"A foursome? You mean three men one after another or three at once?"

"At once."

"That means you took a cock in your ass. You never let me have your ass."

"You never asked for it. Some guys don't like it and I thought you might have been one of them. If you were I wasn't sure how my asking you would go over so I let it go figuring if you wanted it you would ask for it."

She looked at her watch and stood up. "Thank you for the fifteen minutes, Rob. It was important to me that you know I love you. That I didn't do what I did because I no longer cared for you. I'm sorry that I ruined it for us, but don't you ever forget that I love you. Please don't ever forget that."

She had her hand on the door knob when I said, "Misty?"

She turned and I said, "When you get your last thing out of the way call me and we will talk again."

"No, Rob, I'll pass on it. If there is any chance for us I won't do it."

"No. You want to do it, you have been looking forward to doing it and I don't want you looking at me some day down the line and resenting me for preventing it."

"Is this your way of saying we will get back together?"

"No, Misty, it is my way of saying do what you started to do when you suggested that we live together. Finish it and we will talk again."

She stood there looking at me with an unreadable expression on her face and then she turned and left the apartment.

I sat there looking at the door and wondered if maybe we did have a chance. Maybe she had the right idea about getting it all out of your system before you settled down. I pulled out my cellphone and looked up a number on my contact list. I dialed the number and when my call was answered I said:

"Betty Jean? Think you could maybe shake Steve and stop by my place?"

~~The End~~

WANT FREE COPIES OF MY BOOKS?

Just visit my blog and download free copies of my books:

awesomeauthors.org/justplainbob

My other BEST SELLING books available on Amazon!!

Getting Away With Cheating

By: Just Plain Bob

NEW RE-LEASE

Taming Betsy

By: Just Plain Bob

NEW RE-LEASE

Turning Mommies Wild

By: Just Plain Bob

The Playmate

By: Just Plain Bob

NEW RE-LEASE

Married But…

By: Just Plain Bob

In My Wife's Panties

By: Just Plain Bob

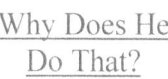

Steamy Swingers

By: Just Plain Bob

Why Does He Do That?

By: Just Plain Bob

Bought And Used

By: Just Plain Bob

The Prodigal Family

By: Just Plain Bob

My Publisher's Other BEST SELLING books on Amazon!!

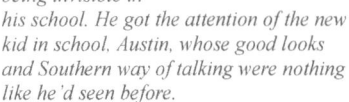

Rough And Raw

By: Chris Johns

Do you have a creative imagination and are into master and slave role playing?

WARNING: Not for the faint of heart. This compilation contains lots of man to man sex, gay romance, and lots of erotic scenes. Read at your own risk.

Resist or Submit

By: Chris Johns

When lines between right and wrong blur, stakes are high and there's more pleasure than hurt…

When the things you know are not always what they seem, friendships become intimate and inhibitions washed away by cravings of the flesh deep inside…
When the awakenings are sudden and struggle is futile…
What will you do? Will you Resist or Submit?

Fighting My Instincts

By: Angus MacGregor

Eighteen-year-old Dylan has a huge secret, and his mother just found out about it!

Will Dylan be able to follow the "straight path" and survive in the most dangerous place he could possibly be in - a camp full of irresistible hot guys trying to desperately deny that they want each other?

In Close Quarters

By: Angus MacGregor

In a business flight to DFW, Frank finds it unbearable when he suddenly wants to jump the bones of the guy next to him.

…unless of course if he somehow convinces him to join the club - the mile high club.

I Never Kissed A Girl Before

By: Miranda Mars

When Laura meets tall, beautiful and gorgeous, but difficult Shontay - she wanted her bad.

Determined to go where no girl has

Catfight, Climax, Friends Again

By: Miranda Mars

Laura loves black women, especially one that she can't get… Shontay. Actually, Laura already had Shontay but lost her because of her propensity to run after every black woman in a skirt.

ever gone before with Shontay, can Laura finally come up with erotic schemes to get Shontay's affections?

Shontay is determined to shut Laura down. But what Laura wants, Laura gets.

Check out the list of all my books!

Becoming a Shared Husband, Vol. 1 –

(Suck Me)

Becoming a Shared Husband, Vol. 2 –

(Husbands Who Stray)

Becoming a Shared Husband, Vol. 3 –

(Get even!)

Becoming a Shared Couple, Vol. 1 –

(Steamy Swingers)

Becoming a Shared Couple, Vol. 2 –

(The Share Thing)

Becoming a Shared Couple, Vol. 3 –

(Kathy is Wild)

Erotica Short Stories, Vol. 1 –

(Taboo Desires)

Erotica Short Stories, Vol. 2 –

(Nasty Steps)

Erotica Short Stories, Vol. 3 –

(Married But…)

Erotica Short Stories, Vol. 4 –

(Sizzling 10)

Erotica Short Stories, Vol. 5 –

(In My Wife's Panties)

Erotica Short Stories, Vol. 6 –

(Taboo Unlimited Desires)

Erotica Short Stories, Vol. 7 –

(XXX Stories)

***

I REALLY LOVE Reviews!

If you enjoyed this book, please share the love and don't forget to leave a review on Amazon or the site of any other retailer you purchased this book from!

I highly appreciate your reviews, and it only takes a minute to write & post one. I can't tell you how much this means to me!

You'll find the list of all my books on my Author Central page... just in case you'd like to leave a review for other books of mine you've read but didn't have time to leave a review.

*Amazon Author Central – http://www.amazon.com/Just-Plain-Bob/e/B00N3S8FJO

One Last Thing, For Kindle Readers...

When you turn the page, Kindle will give you the opportunity to rate this book and share your thoughts on Facebook and Twitter. If you enjoyed my writings, would you please take a few seconds to let your friends know about it? Because... when they enjoy they will be grateful to you and so will I.

Thank you!

Just Plain Bob
justplainbob@awesomeauthors.org

WANT FREE COPIES OF MY BOOKS?
Just visit my blog and download free copies of my books:

awesomeauthors.org/justplainbob